Also by Lish McBride

Hold Me Closer, Necromancer

Necromancing the Stone

Firebug

*Pyromantic**

Heads Will Roll (Tor.com Original)

Burnt Sugar (Tor.com Original)

*forthcoming

FREAKS & OTHER FAMILY

Two Stories

Lish McBride

Freaks & Other Family: Two Stories

Book and cover design by Vladimir Verano

ISBN: 978-0-9984032-0-5

Published by Devo-Lish
Seattle, Washington
lishmcbride@gmail.com

I've missed Sam and Ramon. Their friendship, banter, and good hearts are fun to write and I've wanted to get back to them for so long. Sam's story was first drafted for my Patreon followers, and their support basically made this duo ride again, so I'm very grateful for them. Sam and Ramon aren't finished, not by a long shot, though I'm not sure when they'll get their own novel again.

I would like to thank Martha Brockenbrough and Mel Barnes for their editing skills. Kathy Guerra, Kelly Jones, Rachel Steele and Kim Baker for beta reading for me. All mistakes are mine and mine alone. Big thanks to Vladimir Verano for putting this little book together for me. You are all the very best.

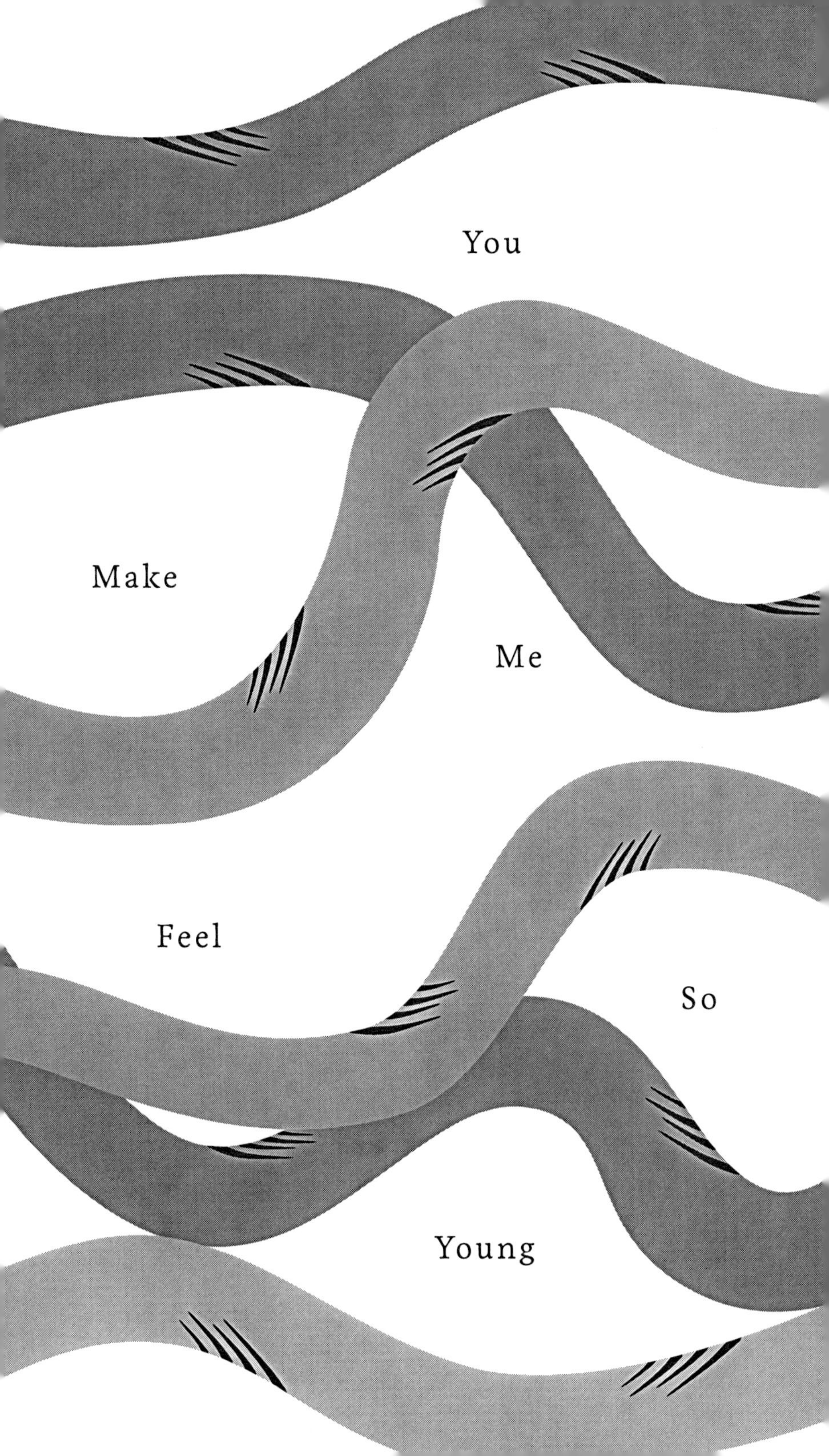
You
Make
Me
Feel
So
Young

We walked in the door and I had to stop myself from tugging at my collar. I wasn't used to black tie. Up until a few months ago, dressing up meant my clothes were clean and didn't have holes. Times had changed, and nothing illustrated that more than me and my friend Ramon escorting my former neighbor, Mrs. Winalski, to a black-tie event. In a ballroom. With actual chandeliers and waiters carrying little plates of unidentifiable food.

"This is weird," I said.

"Weird? Hardly. We're in the midst of eccentric levels of income. They would never be so pedestrian as to be weird." Mrs. W rested one hand on my arm, her other hand snagging a champagne flute off a passing tray. While I looked like I was playing dress up, Mrs. W was the picture of understated elegance. Her gown was a deep, rich red, her silver hair styled up and defying gravity.

"What do you think, Ramon? Weird or eccentric?"

Ramon took a glass of champagne, but didn't drink it. He scanned the room, nostrils flaring slightly. "I'm with Sammy on this one. Definitely weird." He continued to watch the crowd, eyebrows furrowed. "There's a strange smell here, and I get the overwhelming sense that this crowd wants to crack open my bones and drink my youthful marrow."

The crowd in the ballroom was certainly on the older side, well established and wealthy. There were a few exceptions, but most of them looked more like Mrs. W than we did. Jewels flashed, platinum glinted, and some of the outfits would make a substantial payment on my student loans.

Mrs. W clucked her tongue. "That's ageist, Ramon, and quite frankly a little beneath you."

Ramon took a small sip, more to look like he was drinking than anything. "My abuela rules with an iron first. I think very highly of my elders. This isn't about that." His nostrils flared as he took in the scents of the room. "There's just…something about this crowd. I can't tell you more than that."

Mrs. W nodded, placated. "All right, arm candy. Let's circulate and see what we can see." And so we did what I dreaded most—we mingled. Ramon moved with Mrs. W as I made my way across the room and attempted to look approachable. Which meant I didn't have much to do. I'm not intimidating. Mrs. W, however, gives off an air of power and the general impression that you shouldn't mess with her or she'll cut you. And though Ramon appears human, he's not, and people recognize on some level that he can turn into a predator. Me? I'm the kind of guy you hand off your baby to so that you can run to the bathroom. The kind you don't mind taking your daughter out because I'll have her home before curfew. Or at least, I look it.

Harmless.

It's something I've learned to cultivate.

Which is how I ended up working a super secret spy mission at a Bachelor Auction—something I didn't know still existed. I sidled up to a discreet sign off to the side that read, *New Life—bringing resources to those who need it most.* The sign didn't say what those resources might be, or who might be receiving them, and any research we'd attempted had led to a dead end… which was turning out to be a pun. Strange human remains had been discovered—and by strange I mean that we'd found thin, dry husks and nothing else. All that had been left was skin, like people had started spontaneously molting. They were connected somehow to New Life; we just didn't know how.

As I circulated and made small talk, I searched for our other undercover agent. Kell was here somewhere—as a wealthy, handsome single man on the auction block. But despite several circuits of the room, no Kell. Lots of smiles and stares in my direction. An older couple stopped me—her smile wide and toothy, hair pulled back so tight I'm surprised she could blink. Her husband had the same tightly pinched look, only his hair was short and I have no idea what was causing him to look so constipated. His eyes had a sheen to them that made me uncomfortable and reminded me of Ramon's earlier comments about youthful marrow.

"Such a good cause," she said, her smile teetering on shark levels of wide.

I murmured agreement, not that they seemed to be waiting for it.

"Are you part of the auction?" The man asked, the light reflecting a little off his forehead, making his skin look plastic.

"No," I said. "Just here as an escort for a friend."

They tutted at me, their mouths turned down in disappointment. "A nice young man like you? Stuff and nonsense." The woman grabbed my bicep and squeezed, turning the squeeze into a gentle pat.

"I don't think I'm really the type they're looking for—"

I didn't get a chance to finish because the man cut me off. "Stuff and nonsense!" And before I knew it I'd been herded over to a young woman with a headset, and handed over like a wayward lamb.

The woman barely looked at me, spending most of her time staring at her phone and asking me rapid-fire questions as I was guided through a door and into a hallway. I considered arguing with her and explaining that I was not in truth part of the auction, but she didn't seem to care, and it occurred to me that this might work in my favor. I was going into the belly of the beast. I'm not sure why people say that. Nothing good ever happens in the bellies of beasts. If you're there, that means the beast is digesting you and it's game over.

After several turns, sets of stairs, and one release form, I was guided into a room with several other young men whose only common factor seemed to be that they were about my age and wearing tuxes. Most of them seemed excited—a few bewildered, but game. When I asked around, no one knew why we'd been roped into the fun.

Minutes ticked by, the room unbearably warm. Bottles of water were handed out, and conversation died as we all checked our phones. I hadn't had a chance to let Ramon or Mrs W know where I'd gone, so I planned on sending them a message. But my phone had no service. Hopefully Ramon would be able to track my scent down to wherever we were. I was certainly sweating enough to leave a good trail for him to follow.

I pulled at my collar, feeling perspiration bead on my forehead and collecting on the small of my back. I opened the water and took a swig.

It wasn't until the room began to spin that I realized there'd been no snap of a safety seal when I twisted the lid off. I had a split second to regret my lack of attention before I passed out.

I woke up gagged and handcuffed to a chair, which happens to be in the top five worst ways I've ever woken up. Number one still goes to the time I woke up kidnapped and stuck in a cage.

The nice thing about being in this sort of situation on a semi-regular basis is that you don't panic as much. Or maybe that was due to whatever drug cocktail I'd been given. Kell sat across from me, which answered one of my questions. He appeared lucid, his eyes clear, which could not be said for the other people in the room. Most of the other guys were unconscious, and the few who were awake and bleary-eyed were clearly wishing they were still drooling onto their lapels.

Quite frankly, I couldn't blame them. The nice couple that had handed me off to be auctioned away to the highest bidder were at the far end of the room. They were hovering over one of the men who was luckily still unconscious.

"I just don't think this is prudent," the woman said, one hand smoothing her hair. "We should move them—"

The man cut her off with a wave. "I'm not saying we should gorge ourselves, my darling, but what's the harm in a little snack?" He loosened his tie and unbuttoned his shirt. "I'm famished. Aren't you tired of being skin and bones?"

The woman hesitated, staring at the unconscious man in front of them. "Perhaps you're right." She reached up and unlatched her pearls.

As I watched, the woman slid her necklace into her pocket. Her mouth widened, and her lips stretched back farther than any human mouth should extend. Her husband did the same, and then their necks bulged at the base. The bulge rose until their mouths opened wide and a whip-like proboscis snaked out and arched above their heads. The proboscis hovered long enough for me to see the hard, white tooth at the end before it shot into the body of the unconscious man.

A man screamed—I'm not sure which one—but the sound was muffled by his gag. The guy closest to me retched, vomit leaking around the strip of cloth binding his mouth, and I was fervently glad the couple hadn't used duct tape. I hoped he didn't choke.

Someone touched my wrist and I jerked away instinctively before I realized it was Kell. He leaned close. "Don't move. Their vision isn't the best and they're distracted by their feeding."

As Kell picked the lock on my handcuffs, I watched the creatures drink. The proboscis wasn't entirely opaque, and it darkened as fluid moved through it. Their meal began to deflate. It was very much like watching a human Capri Sun. My stomach churned and threatened to reject the appetizers I ate earlier.

"Are they vampires?" I whispered. My arms were suddenly free and Kell moved to get the ones by my feet.

He shook his head. "Blutsauger. Loosely related. They inject a toxin into the bloodstream—it paralyzes and then dissolves the internal organs, flesh, and even bones." With a soft click, my feet were free. "I didn't realize they were still around. Blutsaugern aren't terribly bright and so they aren't the best at hiding their meals. They're not supposed to feed off humans at all. Too visible. Greedy buggers."

Which is about the extent of compassion you could expect from a vampire who also looked at humans as a food source. "I don't suppose you have a plan?"

Kell frowned at the blutsaugern, who were finishing up their meal. There was a sound then, like the death rattle of a milkshake when you've sucked up the last of the ice cream with the straw and start pulling in air.

"Normally, I'd say yes. But I'm ashamed to say that they caught me a little unawares. I didn't expect them, nor did I expect our exact situation. They are terribly strong and their appetites are insatiable. How does 'run like the hounds of hell are chasing you' sound?"

"Define insatiable."

"They won't be able to stop at one. Humans are like Pringles to them."

I stared at him blankly.

He grinned. "Once you pop, you can't stop."

"So glad we're on the same side," I whispered. "I can't in good conscience leave these gentlemen here to be slurped."

"I am open to suggestions, as long at you're quick. They're almost done."

Kell moved onto the guy next to me, quietly unlocking his cuffs while I desperately racked my brain. If Kell was no match for these creatures, then my strength would be considered laughable. Which meant I had to use my brain, which didn't exactly fill me with confidence. I wasn't as bad as Frank under pressure—one time in class his cell phone went off and he ran to the door and chucked it into the hallway instead of turning it off—but I wasn't exactly graceful, either.

Okay. So they're like vampires, but not. What did I know about vampires? What did I have that I could use as a weapon on them? And then I remembered this one time I'd accidentally touched Kell in a boat—which sounded much more salacious than it was—and I had an idea.

"When you say similar, are they close enough that I would have any sort of…leverage against them?" It had been a topic we'd both been avoiding, and now I was wishing I'd brought it up before now.

Kell paused as he stared thoughtfully at the blutsaugern, who were now licking their lips, their proboscises pulled back into hiding. Their flesh had filled in, both of their faces now plumper than they were before. They also looked about ten years younger. I guess we were the resources being distributed by the New Life organization *to* the New Life organization.

"It's worth trying." He resumed his work. "And I can't think of anything better."

Great. Now we had a loose, improbable plan. It was also a problematic plan. Blutsaugern were stronger than Kell physically, or at least two of them together were. We had no idea whether they were stronger magically. They had a long reach and a deadly, toxic sting. So if I wanted to implement my plan, I needed to get close, and I needed blood. I didn't know how to make any of those things happen. Basically, I was screwed, which was oddly reassuring. This right here was my comfort zone.

"Do you have a knife?" I whispered.

"No. Why would I need one?" He pointed at himself. "Vampire." He finished unlocking the guy next to me and moved to the next one. "If anyone here needed a knife, it would be the necromancer."

I looked around the room. Nothing. No knives, no scissors, no sharp-edged chairs. Just passed out dudes, tuxes, and what appeared to be boxes of extra napkins and table linens.

"What if you bit me?"

"No."

Kell didn't elaborate. I double-checked my pockets. All I had was Mrs. W's invite. It would have to do.

It turns out it's actually kind of difficult to give yourself a paper cut on purpose, or at least I had a hard time doing it. The paper was thick and expensive which didn't help either. After several passes I managed to break skin, a fine line of blood welling to the surface. I dug at it with my nails, trying to get more, which hurt like hell. Once my fingers were coated, I dipped down, closed my eyes and touched the floor.

Power snapped. The temperature dropped. Ice flooded my veins and I slowly stretched to my full height.

I've had a lot to learn since I found out what I was and my life went sideways. During that time, I've scrambled to catch up, and I've screwed up a lot. But I'm finally getting the hang of things. And you know what? I'm getting kind of good at my job. I don't look like much. I'm not tough and strong like Ramon and Brid. I don't look powerful and wise like my Mom or Mrs. W. And that's exactly why I was doing so well. People and creatures constantly underestimate me.

So I stood and I smiled and I waited for the blutsaugern to look my way. Then I waved a bloody finger back and forth in a *tsk tsk* motion.

The creatures hissed, their eyes flaring black, the pupil eating up all of the white until there was nothing left.

I took in a deep breath, letting my air out slowly as I commanded my magic to expand. The magic flowed, like a stream, then a gushing river. It moved around all of the humans and I nudged it around Kell when it instinctively reached for him. My magic didn't want to comply—Kell was our kind of creature—but I slammed my will against it.

When my power hit the blutsaugern, the river surged up and in—through their ears, eyes, nostrils and mouths. I smiled and the creatures screamed as I reached down into them and grabbed for what was mine to command. For a brief, wonderful moment, I knew what it was to be the most powerful being in the room. And then my hold slipped and my smile fell. Whatever passed for a blutsaugern soul, it didn't feel like a normal spirit. It was … oily. Hard to grasp. And it surprised me for a second. Which gave the creatures just enough time to slip away and run right at me.

And that was when I noticed my second really stupid mistake of the evening. I'd failed to draw a circle. In my rush, it simply hadn't occurred to me. Which meant I had zero protection against the extremely deadly creatures coming my way.

I can now cross "getting tackled by two angry blutsaugern" off my bucket list. I've never been hit by a speeding car, but imagine the feeling is similar. The impact threw me back, knocking over empty chairs and several unconscious guys. While it didn't feel great, the guys did at least break my fall and probably saved me from significant injury. Not that it mattered. The creatures were on me and they were more than happy to continue their feast.

The male blutsauger leaned forward, ripping my shirt open down the front. Buttons popped and flew, pinging into the darkness. There went my deposit. James was going to murder me when he saw the state of my tux. He'd wanted me to get my own—I had argued that it would be cheaper to rent. And now we were going to have to replace it. Having to pay so much for what James saw as an inferior suit would just add to his indignation. If the blutsaugern really did manage to kill me, James would probably hire another necromancer to bring me back so he could yell at my attentive corpse.

I watched as the creatures grinned and their throats bulged. When their proboscises unfurled, I broke into a cold sweat. This was it. This was how I was going to die. A stupid human juice box because I couldn't take two seconds to draw a damn circle.

I reached up and held onto the necklace I always had around my neck—the one my mom made me with my protective pouch nestled next to the old silver coin Ed had given me. I squeezed the pouch and thought about my mom. Haley, my sister. All of my friends. I though about Brid. I wished them goodbye as a tiny, gooey bit of mucus dripped onto my stomach.

"Sam!" Kell practically growled my name as he popped up behind the blutsaugern with a folding chair. "Your necklace!"

Then he wacked the creatures with the chair, doing every professional wrestler who ever lived, proud.

While Kell selflessly threw himself at deadly creatures in the name of distraction, I tried to figure out what the hell he was talking about. He couldn't mean my pouch. All that did was hide my powers from the kinds of things interested in necromancers—ghosts, dead things, other necromancers and the like.

That left me with the coin. I reached up and touched it with my bloody hand to get a better look at it. To be honest I hadn't gotten around to figuring out what the damn thing did. But the second I touched it, I finally understood what Ed had meant when he'd handed it to me after Douglas's death. I was supposed to feed it. At the time, I hadn't known what I was supposed to feed it *with.*

Turns out blood worked fine. And my blood was better than fine. I held the coin and it drank my blood quickly, starved from so long without a feeding. The small silver disk in my palm was a chasm of want. An infinite pinpoint of hunger. And if it liked blood, it was going to like blutsauger soul a hell of a lot more.

I rolled, grabbing the woman's leg. She was wearing stockings, but there was a long tear up one of the calves. I slapped the coin against the woman's skin and slammed all of my will onto the coin followed by a single command. *Feed.*

She thrashed, almost like she was having a seizure. I held tight, keeping the coin against her flesh. As she struggled, I felt the oilslick of her soul slip into the coin. Then she collapsed on me, all dead weight. At least, I think she was dead weight. I touched her skin, closing my eyes. Yup. She was gone.

I crawled out from under her, making my way over to Kell, who had one hand on the other creature's chest, and the other holding the proboscis away from him like it was a venomous snake. Once I got close enough, I was stuck. They were moving too fast for me to get a good shot in, and I didn't want to hit Kell with the coin. It was a little overzealous, and I wasn't sure I could keep it from attacking my fellow Council member.

As I tried to figure out what to do next, there was a large crack as someone or something crashed against the door. I turned to look. Kell and Mr. Blutsauger didn't seem to notice. Another crash, this time denting the door. I hobbled over, flipped the lock and threw the door open just as Ramon flew past me and crashed into the opposite wall. He looked a little stunned as he straightened up.

I pointed at the bloodsucker wrestling match going on behind me. "Help Kell. I need you to hold the creature still for two seconds." Ramon nodded and ran toward it, his suit starting to tear along the seams. He was dangerously close to changing, which wouldn't help us much. "And don't let that stinger tooth thing touch you!"

I wasn't sure he heard me as he barreled into the thing, grabbing the body away from Kell, though the vampire kept hold of the proboscis. When I got close enough, I slammed the coin against the creature's neck. I didn't even have to tell the coin this time. It slurped up the oily soul with no word from me. Which meant after one meal, it was making decisions on its own. Icy power crashed through my system. Later. I'd worry about the creepy, possibly sentient coin later. Probably when everything stopped spinning and twirling. The room started to narrow as the edges of my vision blackened. I thought, *that can't be good* right before the lights went out completely.

"Your eyes rolled up in your head and you hit the ground," Mrs. W said, pulling her coat tighter. It was late and the air had a definite chill to it.

I was sitting off to the side, sipping water and icing the goose egg on the back of my skull. The parking lot was a sea of flashing lights and emergency personnel. Even though my necklace was shoved into my pocket, Kell was sitting well outside of reaching distance. Ramon stood next to Mrs. W, eyes scanning the parking lot.

"I tried to grab you," Ramon said. "But my arms were full of…whatever that was."

"Any guesses on what happened?" I traded my empty water bottle to Ramon for a new one. The safety seal gave a reassuring crack.

"Imagine that you are a conduit," Kell said holding one hand out in a C shape. "When your blood hit the coin, it completed the circuit." He brought his hands together making a circle. "The coin draws power in, it cycles through you. Then it goes either back into the coin, finishing the cycle, or you push it out, grounding it." He gave me a flat look. "Unless your name is Sam. Then for some reason you keep the power flowing into you and you don't move it out in either direction. Power slams though fast—" He pulled his hands apart. "Too fast, too much. The breaker, which is you, flips." Kell spread his hands flat. "Then you collapse onto the floor like a debutante in a too-tight corset."

I took a long sip as I thought about that. "I didn't know what the coin would do."

Kell stared at me. "You've been wearing a Stygian coin around your neck and you have no idea what it does?"

I felt my cheeks flush with embarrassment, and though it was dark, I'm sure Kell noticed. Vampires are always aware of blood, and it was pooling nicely in my face. "I've been busy. Anyway, this kind of thing happens to me all the time."

"It's true," Ramon said. "It's getting to the point that we're afraid to let him outside. He's a trouble magnet."

"Make time," Kell said.

I opened my mouth, but Mrs. W cut me off. "He's right, Sam. Make time. Or delegate. Have Frank look things up. It's his job. Or James."

"Frank's busy with the gnomes and James is always busy keeping us all from, well, things like this."

Kell held one finger in front of my face. "No excuses." He held up a second finger. "Do better." Another finger. "And don't wear something when you *have no idea what it does.*"

"Yes, sir." I adjusted the cold pack. "What's going to happen to all of them?" I nodded to the rest of the drugged bachelors in the parking lot. It hurt to move my head, and I winced.

"We're spinning this as best we can," Mrs. W said. "We hid the bodies, such as they were. We're letting that couple, the Schmetterlings, take the fall. The police will think that they've cut and run. As for why they would drug and tie-up a bunch of young men, we're letting law enforcement draw their own conclusions on that one. Whatever they come up with, I'm pretty sure it won't be "obscure vampire-like creatures tried to eat half of a bachelor auction."

"The Schmetterlings?" I asked.

"That was the alias the creatures were using," Kell said. "It means 'butterfly' in German."

"Makes sense," I said, as the police made their way over and collected my statement.

I went through our heavily abbreviated and somewhat vague tale. Any holes in the story would likely be attributed to the fact that I'd been drugged for part of the evening. After I gave them my contact info and the medics checked me out, I was allowed to go. Ramon was instructed to keep an eye on me, even though I didn't have a concussion.

Kell decided to hang around—he felt someone from the Council should stick close just incase anything else popped up that needed handling. We said our goodbyes and parted ways. I tried to walk on my own to Mrs. W's car, but Ramon got tired watching me wobble like a baby deer and scooped me up and carried me.

I grinned at him. "Take me to bed or lose me forever."

"I can't believe you're Top Gun-ing me right now. We almost died."

"I'm going to blame the head injury," I said, patting his chest. "You're supposed to say, 'show me the way home, honey.'"

"I will do no such thing, and you can't blame it on the head injury, because you say those kinds of things to me all the time."

"This is true. Let's go on a crime spree then, and we'll blame *that* on the head injury."

"You can't even walk. We need to get you home so you can rest," Ramon said firmly.

"Yeah, so we can then explain to James how we both managed to completely ruin the top-of-the-line tuxedo rentals we're wearing." Top-of-the-line to me. James had sneered openly at them before throwing up his hands in despair, which wouldn't stop him from berating us. If anything, I think he'd find it more insulting somehow, and the fact that we'd ruined only semi-decent tuxes instead of really nice tuxes would just be salt in the wound.

Ramon paused as we both thought that over. Mrs. W pulled ahead of us, fishing her keys out of her clutch.

"Shit," Ramon said. "I hadn't thought about that."

We both stared out into the night, silent as we contemplated our impending dooms.

"Head injury," we both said at the same time.

"We can definitely blame the suits on that."

"And if he doesn't buy it," Ramon added, "then you can just pass out again."

"Deal."

The way Mrs. W drove, it was likely I'd pass out again soon anyway, and then Ramon would be left to explain everything to an infuriated James.

"You boys buckled up?" She asked.

"We are," Ramon said. "Show us the way home, Mrs. W."

"My pleasure," she said, right before she slammed the car into gear and hit the gas. The fact that the cops were nearby didn't stop her from driving like she was on the Formula One circuit. I huddled into my seat and felt very, very old.

Halfway Through the Wood

I rested my hands on the steering wheel, listening to the tick of the rapidly cooling engine, along with the various tings, pops, and hisses that came with the car settling down. My car had been so quiet before my accident. I would have maybe heard the engine cooling. But now my car is downright chatty, like my uncle Héc after one too many cervezas, or my sister Selena all the time.

I'd never considered my life as *quiet*—you don't live in a small house with three younger siblings, a mother who loves show tunes, and with a horde of nosy aunts and uncles living nearby to qualify for quiet. But I now know that was what it had been. Quiet. Like Rice Krispies before you add the milk. Except it wasn't just the noise. It was every single sense.

I could smell the lazy heat coming off the asphalt, lingering scent traces of my girlfriend, Dessa, and the sweet cinnamon and banana of the bread sitting wrapped next to me. Since we were in the last throes of summer, the sun was still up. Soon the nights would lengthen, the darkness coming earlier. Not that it mattered to me much anymore. My night vision was now excellent, so even if it hadn't been daylight, I would have been able to see movement at the far end of the block telling me that Mr. Walsh had already crept outside to sneak a cigarette where his wife wouldn't catch him. Of course the whole neighborhood knew Mrs. Walsh was well aware, a fact Mr. Walsh was oblivious to. I heard the snap of his lighter and smelled faint traces of tobacco and smoke even from here.

Overwhelming data streams in and I still struggled to sort it all. Sometimes I had to stop, pause, focus and breathe so I could get a handle. Metal whined and I quickly let go of the steering wheel. That was the biggest thing I had to remember—without thinking about it I could braid my steering wheel into a wreath. I could probably toss my car. I let out a shuddering breath. No, that wasn't the biggest thing. What I really had to be careful about was not getting stressed out and turning into a bear. I don't mean that in a figurative sense. I mean actually turning into a bear. To be specific, a grizzly bear. And nothing said calm and relaxing like hanging out with extended family for your abuela's birthday party.

I couldn't skip it. Not if I ever want my abuela to speak to me again. I'd already missed several dinners and family events. I'd missed my little cousin's choir recital, and I was noticeably absent during the pre-dinner tamale prep. And I can't remember the last time I'd taken abuela to Mass. If I missed her birthday dinner, I was dead. I took a deep, settling breath and opened my car door.

As I stepped out I inhaled the sharp scent of pine, and heard the rustle of what smelled like possum in one of the neighbor's trashcans. If so, he was up early. Possums are nocturnal, but lots of animals got screwed up in urban environments. My palms started to sweat. I could do this. I needed to do this.

I loved my abuela and my dad's side of the family and it felt weird to dread their presence. They'd always been a source of comfort, even after my dad left and remarried, I still only felt warmth and love being around them. Sure, we could be loud. We squabbled. But underneath that was the feeling that—no matter what—family came first. I'd never understood how my dad could walk away from that. Divorce was practically unheard of on that side of my family, so he knew what the repercussions would be. Still, he'd tried at first to stick around, I'll give him that. But after watching what his random visits did to my sisters and my mom, over and over, I just couldn't take it anymore. I told him not to come back. No one was more surprised than me that he listened.

I focused on putting one foot in front of the other as I made my way to the front door. After my change, distance had been necessary. I didn't have the best control, and I was afraid I'd hurt someone, or accidentally expose what I was. I'd made all kinds of excuses. I was busy with school, sick, working, and my family had cut me some slack. Up to a point. And I'd reached that point. Much longer and family would start "dropping by" to check on me. I lived with my friend Sam in a house with living lawn gnomes, killer landscaping, and ghosts. Even my very human family would notice something was off.

I could hear the chatter of voices and the strum of several guitars, all of which was quickly drowned out by the warbling blast from a trombone. My little cousin Joey had just joined band in school. For his parents' sake, I sent up a short prayer that he would get better. Fast.

I stepped up to the door and closed my eyes, centering myself. Waiting wasn't going to make it any easier. I reached for the handle only to have the door opened for me. Surprise turned quickly to joy as I saw my uncle Héc, who wasted no time pulling me into a hug that took me off my feet. My uncle was the baby of the family, a late in life one, and so was closer to an older brother than an uncle, really, especially after my dad left. He'd stepped in to help my mom out with us, and normally I wouldn't have gone so long without seeing him. He wouldn't have let me, but he wasn't even married a year yet, and his new wife had him a little distracted. When Héc finally did put me down, I saw the smiling face of Rene, my newest auntie.

"Don't keep him all to yourself, Héctor. He's my favorite nephew, too." Rene is originally from Georgia, and her accent is liquid and beautiful, but sounded much slower in family gatherings. Spanish is a very fluid language, fast and musical. And I think Rene slowed her speech down even more in group settings like this, first so my abuela could parse through her accent easier, and also because I think she found the juxtaposition of the two language speeds to be funny.

Rene was, well, gorgeous. She has good cheekbones, a wide smile, and her sun-kissed brown hair has some wave to it. She was also, as my uncle put it, tall and "built to kick ass."

"We don't have favorites in the Hernández clan, sweetheart." Héc said, sternly.

Rene rolled her eyes. "Sure you don't." She gave me a big squeeze. "I've heard you've had yourself a bit of a year."

"You could say that." And she only knew the half of it—Brooke's death, Sam's inheritance, and my "sickness," not to mention college classes, switching my major, and dating Dessa. Rene gave me an extra squeeze. I'd been worried when they'd first started dating. Uncle Héc was amazing and we spent so much time together, what if I didn't like his Rene? I knew from the first second he started talking about her that she was special to him. His face softened and his voice changed when he spoke about her. My sisters and I spent several weeks fretting about it and shamelessly looking her up on social media. We were all happy for my uncle, but we also had all judgment cannons locked and loaded.

Then I'd been invited over to his place for dinner and Rene had said, "Héctor is, of course, cooking. Much to my mama's eternal shame, I am a disaster in the kitchen unless it involves the grill. But I can beat your uncle at arm wrestling, so there's that." And it was just impossible for me not to like her. My sisters were won over just as easily.

Rene pulled back to get a good look at me and that's when I noticed that her smile had faltered a fraction and her pupils had dilated…and then the scent hit me. I can only blame the delay on distraction and my learning curve—there were a lot of scents to parse out in the house. But there is was. Underneath the scent of food, family, and my abuela's little ankle-biter, Mimi, the heady musk that told me Rene wasn't exactly human. Rene was a were.

"You *have* been busy." She straightened my collar, running her fingers down the lapels as her nostrils flared. Rene was trying to figure out what I was.

I put my hand on hers. "I'll tell you later, I promise."

There was a pinched, worried cast to her face, which she shook off as she let me go with a final once over. "Both of us."

I couldn't quite keep my surprise to myself.

"He knows," she said, looping an arm around his back and pulling him close. "Or I wouldn't have married him."

"Like you could resist my charms," Héc said, grinning down. He gave my cheek a gentle slap. "Come on, you best get on in there."

I followed them deeper into the house, which was full to bursting with family and friends that had earned that status. My family has been known to rope in people who we've decided need food and family or those that simply can't run away fast enough.

I settled my banana bread onto a table already full of cookies and treats. There was another one there already, but we'd need at least two for the crowd.

My mom had brought my sisters over earlier. Despite the rift the divorce had caused, my mom stayed close to the family, even though she didn't always see eye to eye with abuela. My abuela is from Guadalajara, and as such tends to be on the conservative side. If you asked my abuela, my mother's family is full of "liberal heathens." There were a lot of things my mother did and said that caused strife with my abuela. Before the divorce, they butted heads like nobody's business. So you would think the divorce would make everyone happy, but my abuela was furious. It was not a part of her culture and with her religion, the divorce took legitimacy away from my father's offspring, making bastards out of me and my three sisters. You can't bring up my father's name without my abeula's mouth becoming pinched, the pressure causing small white lines by her nostrils. It was a sight.

So post-divorce, both sides tread lightly. My mom may not agree with grandmother's views, but she does her best to be respectful. In return, abuela isn't openly hostile about my mother's choices. They've managed a somewhat grudging acceptance of each other. It's made things easier on us, so my mom made the effort. I was still surprised to see her at the party. Her arm was slung around my sister Selena's shoulders, in her other hand she held a sweating glass tumbler. I could smell the limes and the sharp bite of tequila from here.

I kissed her cheek. "If Aunt Mari made that, you should probably give your keys to Rosa, Mamá."

My mom snorted. "That's why I'm only having one."

"One is enough."

My mamá huffed, but handed off her keys to my oldest sister, Rosa. I hadn't caught sight of my other sister Gabi yet, but she'd surface eventually. I circulated, hugging family, whirling baby cousins around, and basking in the sensory overload that was family. I hadn't realized how much my self-imposed isolation had been bugging me until now. It was like the blood rushing into a limb that had fallen asleep. Hearing, smelling, seeing—and in the case of my Uncle Fernando who'd just smoked a cigar, practically tasting—my family had sparked that dead part of me back to life.

I soaked up their presence like it was finals week and they were my first cup of coffee. I felt loved and warm and full—of food, of laughter, of everything that was important for life. My family interrogated me about Dessa, how school was going, and what I was doing for work. My sisters had told everyone that I wasn't flipping burgers anymore, and telling them that I was assisting Sam was a non-job and wouldn't go over well. So I told them part of the truth—I was looking into getting work at a small private clinic in Issaquah. I just didn't tell them that my bosses would be werewolves.

I found my abuela holding court on the back porch. Strings of fairy lights, crepe paper and balloons cast colors all along the back of the house, including my abuela's wicker throne. I brought my abuela another glass of wine, her perfume strong in my nostrils, and I felt content. Everything was going great. I'd spent all that time fretting over nothing.

She took the glass, patting my cheek fondly. "We missed you in Mass." Even though she'd lived half of her life here, she still had a fairly thick accent. It gave her words a richness that they would have lacked, like the difference between those packets of grainy instant hot cocoa and hot chocolate my mom made at home using real chocolate. After you've had a sip of the real thing—smooth sweetness, followed by the warmth of cinnamon and and the bite of cayenne, it's hard to go back to those packets.

"I know," I said, and I didn't have to fake my contrition. I may not be a practising Catholic, but I hate disappointing her. If getting dressed up and sitting for hours on a hard wooden pew would make her happy, then I would do it. The crowd would likely drive me nuts and the incense would be a problem, but I'd make the effort for her. "What if I take you Sunday? I'll drive and after I'll come back for brunch." Brunch would stretch into dinner for sure, and it was likely I'd be giving up my entire Sunday.

She patted my cheek again, this time with a faint hint of command. "And bring your new girl with you. I want to meet her." It wasn't up for debate. I could only hope that Dessa would be willing. "Now get me some the shrimp Rene just took of the grill, and another helping of the salmon, will you? And get yourself a burger. You're too skinny."

"Por supuesto, abuelita." I straightened up and looked along the long table set on the porch—you could barely see the tablecloth under all the food—trying to find the plates. The weather was perfect for an outside party, my little cousin had stopped playing his trombone, so good music filled the air, a rhythmic counterpoint to all the laughter and conversation, and my heart felt full.

You know that scene in movies where someone walks into a party and the music suddenly stops? It's great for dramatic effect, but I'd never thought it to be very realistic. But apparently it does occasionally happen. The conversation petered out first, except for the joyous screeching of my little cousins as they chased each other around the yard. Then the music faltered and trailed off. It was a real shame that crickets don't do well in Seattle, because they would have been perfect now. As it was, all we had was Mimi's sharp little Pomeranian barks to let us all know that a stranger was here.

I didn't drop my plate at the sight of my padre standing just outside the sliding doors to my abuela's porch. He stood stiffly, as if his short sleeve button up and jeans had been starched, his arm resting around a slim brunette about ten years his junior. I look like my father—a little taller, but my build was slimmer until my change. I have my mother's mouth and eyes, but the rest is all Hernández. He'd put on a few pounds since I last saw him. He had his chin out, shoulders back, and his eyes practically burned with challenge. Bears are not territorial. Not really. But humans are, and the human in me wanted in on the challenge he was so clearly issuing.

The woman didn't have the same bearing. Her shoulders were slightly curled in, and she'd dipped her head so that her bangs slid forward to hide her eyes. She looked delicate, like she'd startle at the loudest noise, or crumble in on herself any minute. I could see the slight tremble in her hand as she put it on her stomach. Her belly was rounded, and judging from the experience of multiple pregnancies of aunties and my own mother, I'd say she was about seven months along, but that was a guess. Some women show more than others.

Even from here I could smell them—my father still wore the same cologne. I expected her to wear perfume for some reason, but I didn't smell any. Probably had to stop wearing it when she got pregnant. Some women become sensitive to smells. I got a hint of baby powder—likely from her deodorant—and the acrid bite of fear. Though she was trying to hide it, she was terrified to be here. Between the two of them there was a lot of fear and self-righteous anger in one place.

My pulse quickened in response. The plate shattered in my hand. I quickly released my grip on what was left in the hopes that everyone would think I'd dropped it.

I finally caught sight of my sister Gabi—her eyes round with shock, my other sisters quickly pulling her between them. They all looked to me, instinctively. My mamá was a mighty force, but when it came to my padre, it was my job to jump in, to protect them. All of them. My heart beat the rapid tattoo of an overwrought organ. I felt the sweat bead my brow, my lip, and a lone drop slid down my spine. My hands itched, and my knuckles felt thick. None of these were good signs.

This was bad. Really, really bad. My control, considering my fairly new status and youth, was pretty good. But I had topped out on stress. I was hoping for a few things: that my padre wouldn't notice me and force a confrontation and that no one else would notice that I was shaking and sweating like I had the flu. The first could end with me getting physical, which meant I could accidentally chuck my padre through a fence or worse. The second was unlike me, usually, and would raise eyebrows. I was calm. I took things in stride. I did not freak out and pound furniture into kindling. But I wasn't sure I would be able to pull off the human act much longer.

It was Rene and Héc that saved me, really. My tío pushed a cold bottle against the back of my neck, startling me. When I whirled around, he calmly pushed the wedge of a lime into the beer and handed it to me, then did the same for his own. He gave me a wink. While I was processing this, Rene pressed a burger into my hand. I smelled lime, cilantro, and the rich tang of the beef.

“Eat.” Her command was soft, but there was solid authority in it, and I unthinkingly obeyed. “It’s a new recipe. Carne asada burger. I’m trying to do a fusion thing. So eat it all or you’ll hurt my feelings.” The spell was broken and, while not calm, I was at least back in control. I washed the burger down and watched as all hell broke loose. My tiny abuela flew out of her chair, her Spanish so rapid fire that even I was having a hard time following along. Not to be outdone, my aunties jumped in, everyone trying to be louder than everyone else.

In the midst of this, my sisters stood quietly in a tiny knot, my mother standing mutely behind them. The shock would wear off soon and they would likely join in on the yelling. I left my empty bottle on the table, squeezed Rene’s hand in thanks, and slid around the outside of the crowd.

No one noticed as I pulled my sisters and my mamá out of the shouting match and through the side gate of the house. I looked back as I turned to latch the gate. My padre still stood rigid, his chin up, but his wife appeared crumpled, the weight of all the animosity pushing her closer to him. I pulled the gate closed and left.

“I didn’t know,” Selena said. “Did any of you know?” We were all squished into the small kitchen of our madre’s house. We hadn’t discussed it, but we’d all headed back here to regroup. Mamá, her hands steady, but brow furrowed, was pulling left overs out of the fridge for us. I was grateful for this since I hadn’t been at the party long enough to really dig into the food. My stomach mourned the loss of my abuela’s birthday tamales and Rene’s grilled salmon. There wouldn’t be any left by Sunday.

Gabi shook her head mutely while Rosa yanked plates out of the cupboards. My sisters all glanced at me. "I haven't talked to him since he left." They knew this, but apparently they needed to hear it again. No one needed to question Mamá. He'd stopped trying to talk to her years ago when she made it clear that she'd wanted nothing to do with him by sending all of his checks back torn up into confetti in small white envelopes. We could have used that money, but we were all too proud to take it.

"Of all the bone-headed things," my mother said, setting down the foil wrapped platter a little too hard on the table. She let out a frustrated whoosh of air before turning to the oven to preheat it. My mom refused to microwave empanadas. She felt that it made them "squishy." Mamá had been taking cooking classes—Greek this time—and so the meal spread out before us was a glorious clashing of cultures. Empanadas sat next to a cucumber salad with feta and olives. Hummus and pita bread were accompanied by homemade salsa. It didn't really matter—it would all be delicious. My sisters were just staring at it dejectedly anyway.

"You didn't even get to tell them your news." Rosa rested a hand on Mamá's shoulder, and Mamá covered her hand with one of her own.

I started filling up my plate. Emotional turmoil aside, I need food and lots of it. "What news?"

"Paul asked Mamá to marry him," Selena said softly. Her eyes were fierce, a clear demand issued in them as to how I was to respond. "He's asked us all to move in with him."

Paul is my mother's boyfriend. I'd spent some time with him, but didn't really know him like my sisters did. He was a history professor at the college Mamá taught at. Quiet. Reserved. He looked like a displaced Viking in jeans and a suit jacket. I wasn't sure about him at first because he was one of those guys who didn't really emote much. He didn't say or do anything wrong, I just couldn't get a read on him. After they'd been dating a short time, we all went out to dinner to celebrate my mother's birthday. Paul met us at the restaurant. He didn't see us at first as we walked up. Paul was turned slightly away, nervously clutching a bouquet of tulips, my mom's favorite flowers. I knew the exact moment he saw Mamá. Paul smiled and lit up, like my mom was the spark that set his soul on fire.

I gave Mamá the response that she needed, which luckily was also the one I wanted to give. "I am so happy for you, Mamá." I got up and hugged her close, careful not to squeeze too tight.

"Mamá was going to tell abuelita tonight," Rosa said with a sad smile.

"I promised to take her to Mass Sunday," I said, shifting back so I could look my mom in the eye. "Why don't we all go and you can tell her at brunch?"

My mom agreed, liking the idea, though I knew she enjoyed going to Mass about as much as she enjoyed getting a root canal. Everyone calmed down a little as we started filling plates and Mamá put the empanadas in the oven to warm.

"I can't believe he ruined abuela's birthday," Selena said, popping a dolmade into her mouth.

And then my sister Gabi burst into tears. Selena kept her distance but patted Gabi's back, a look of abject panic on her face. The rest of us shoved paper towels at her because none of us can handle Gabi crying.

As a reintroduction back into normal family life, it was going about as well as I'd hoped.

❖

I hit the ramp when I got home. My friend Sam had built a half pipe in the yard as a gift to me for when I recovered from my accident. He felt some major guilt because I was infected trying to save him. I've been doing my best to dispel that guilt. First, Sam has been my best friend forever. Of course I'd risk my life to save his. That wasn't even a question in my mind. Second, I actually *like* being a bear. It has its downsides of course. But it's hard to not enjoy a stronger, faster, tougher me. I'm like Ramon 2.0.

I dropped onto the ramp, letting go of the day as I felt the board under my feet, the warm evening air swirling as I went. After a few passes, I popped my truck up onto the coping, catching my breath in an axle stall. That was when I spotted Sam sitting across from me on the other side of the ramp. He sat with his knees up, watching quietly. I gave him a curt nod, then popped off the coping and back onto the ramp.

There are a lot of things that I like about Sam. He's loyal, smart and brave and doesn't actually think he's any of those things. And he's good with silence. Sam won't push unless he thinks I want him to. If I talk, he'll be the first to listen, but in moments like this, he'll simply sit and let me be. I wish I could say I was the same, but I'm not. I push like hell. But then, that's the friend that Sammy needs. He needs a little shove sometimes.

I'm careful on the ramp. My human self altered slightly with the change. I have more muscle. I'm denser and my center of gravity seems to have shifted. Tricks that I mastered years ago have to be remastered. In a moment of muscle memory I can forget about my strength and I've broken several boards landing with too much force.

When I finally take a break, I'm sweaty and winded, but I feel better. My mind is clearer and my heart less crazed. I'm ready for Sammy. He wordlessly hands me a bottle of water, and we both size the other up while pretending we aren't doing just that. Sam out of guilt and concern, me just out of concern. My friend has taken on a lot this year. He hasn't said anything, but I know he's not sleeping well. His face is pinched, his eyes bruised and he smiles less. If I catch him when he thinks no one is looking, he looks lost.

"It's funny that you still wear a helmet."

I sit next to him, dangling my legs over the ramp. "Healing head wounds sucks and I don't have time for a concussion."

"But if you got a concussion, I could take care of you and wake you up every hour and it would be super romantic and shit." He handed me a second bottle. "You go to your grandma's party?"

I nod, but he doesn't continue. Now Sam will wait to see if I want to talk about it, or if we want to be stereotypically manly and bottle up our feelings. We are badasses at times, but we are not the manliest of men in a traditional sense. Don't get me wrong—when faced with adversity, we'll still bring it. We'll lift our chins, put up our fists, and throw ourselves into unbeatable odds, even when we know it's an unwinnable situation. We drink beer, eat steak—or at least I do. Sam's a vegetarian. But beyond skateboarding, I don't really care about sports. I think it's good to talk things out, and I don't subscribe to the idea that there is only one way to be a man. "It sucked," I said, finally. "And I didn't get any tamales."

"That is a crime."

I laugh, and it sounds wet and suspiciously close to a sob. I press the heels of my hands to my eyes. After a long moment counting the stars on the backs of my eyelids, I tell him everything. "He just walked in, Sammy. Proud. Spine straight, like he was the wronged one. Like we were all hurtful bastards. Like we were the ones who left him behind."

"Dickish, for certain. I'm sure in his mind, that's how it is. Your dad—" he stops and shakes his head. "He never deserved you guys. I think you were all too much for him, and he knew it. I know it hurt like hell, but him leaving was the best thing that happened to any of you."

"Thanks." I let go of my board and watch as it slides smoothly down the ramp, back and forth, each pass getting shorter and shorter until it stops. "And why now? Why like this?"

I didn't actually expect an answer, but Sammy gave me one anyway. "Because it's about him, not about you guys." He paused and I knew he was weighing his words carefully. "I don't know his new wife, obviously, but the baby…well, it probably was the biggest factor."

I growled, actually growled. "He walked out and he just started over. Who does that? How can you just do over your family, like it's an error on a baseball field?"

"I'm really proud of you for using a sports metaphor. It's like we're real dudes, but they don't actually have "do overs" in real baseball. At least I don't think they do."

I drop my elbows to my knees and lean forward. "You have no idea how shitty this feels—." And I stop myself, but not in time to stop Sammy from giving me a half smile as he waits for me to catch up. "I am an ass."

He shrugged. "Look, it feels different for both of us. I don't really remember my dad. You were older and you do. My mom had my stepdad. Your mom has raised four kids by herself. Both are their own brands of shitty."

I nod again, not really trusting myself to respond.

"I could honestly give a rat's ass about your dad. He can rot. So how you want to handle him, I'm completely behind you on that. But the baby? I know you, buddy. If you ignore that kid, you'll kick yourself for it." He pauses, and I know he's thinking about his own baby half-sisters. "It's something to think about anyway."

And of course he's right, because Sammy knows me like no one else. There is a soft whoosh as the largest crow I've ever seen lands on Sam's shoulder and proceeds to peck him repeatedly on the head. It looks like it hurts.

"Okay, okay, I'm late. I get it. Why can't I get a verbal warning?"

I don't hear the crow respond, but I can tell Sam does. He sighs and gets up, the crow digging into his shoulder to hold on. "I'm apparently being summoned."

"No rest for the wicked," I said, holding out my fist for a bump. He tapped my knuckles gently with his.

"Truer words were never spoken." I can't help but notice how defeated he sounds. I make a mental note to talk to the gnomes to set up a special surprise for him. It's hard to focus on your own misery when garden gnomes toilet paper your bedroom.

Again.

My sister Selena works Sunday evening, and I end up driving her to work so she doesn't have to take the bus. I have a lingering headache from the incense, but Mass went well otherwise and my abuela has been mollified. I find I don't mind the headache.

"Did you see her face when Mamá told her about Paul?" Selena digs through her backpack trying to find her ChapStick so I can't see her smile.

"Could have knocked me over with a feather," I said. I had expected, at best, a forced smile from my abuela at the news of my mother's engagement, but she had been genuinely pleased.

Selena eyed me. "I think it would take more than a feather these days. You lifting weights or something?"

"Or something." Turning into a bear definitely qualifies as other.

Selena finally digs out her ChapStick and the smell of vanilla fills the car as she applies it. "So I've been thinking about it and I've thought of the perfect baby gift for Papa."

We've pulled up to a red light, so I'm able to treat her comment with a good, long stare of incredulity.

"What?" she says. "I can be nice."

I snort, which is about what she expects from me. Selena actually is kind and giving—if she likes you. If you make her mad, stay out of her way.

"We could get them a lovely framed photo of all of us giving Papa the finger."

I laugh then—I can't help it. Because I can imagine that photo quite clearly. Gabi would do it, but you would be able to tell it was done grudgingly and only to please us. Rosa wouldn't smile, but her hand would be steady. Selena would be grinning like a maniac, both dimples clear, and both hands in front of her, the middle finger extended proudly. "Mamá would kill us."

"Even if we gift wrap it really nice and get a good frame?"

"Even if."

Selena slouches in her seat and we both say, "I raised you better than that" in unison, though my sister sounds much more like Mamá than I do.

"We have to do something." Selena crosses her arms, not pouting, because she would never do that. She looks angry, but I know my sister well. She's hurt. Papa's actions have thrown salt in a raw wound, reminding my sister that there'd been no father daughter dance at her Quinceañera. He hadn't been at her graduation—he hadn't even sent a card. Yes, I'd told him to stop coming by, but he could have tried to hit the milestones. He could have tried, period. He hadn't even pretended to fight for us.

"I wonder if he's having a girl."

My heart lurches and I reach over and squeeze my sister's hand. "I'll handle it." I say, and because I want to see her smile I add, "I know a good frame shop."

It's a week later, and I'm suddenly doubting my decision. Héctor doesn't say anything as he takes the present from me, the pastel paper wrinkled from my grip. I'd almost ruined Gabi's beautiful wrapping job. I can't make my leg stop tapping.

Rene is drinking sweet tea and enjoying the show. "I always thought bears were calmer."

"I'd love to point out the short comings of you being a lynx, but I'm afraid my general ignorance of the animal is keeping me from doing so." But I give her a tough bear glare to tell her how much I appreciate the mockery.

"Very scary." A soft half smile twists her lips and she refills my own cup of sweet tea, insisting that it will make me feel better. Personally, I think sweet tea is kind of weird, but you don't tell someone from Georgia that *ever*. It's the only time I've really seen Rene angry.

"Do you know you hum show tunes when you're nervous?"

I nod at her. "Which one was it?"

"That one from Sound of Music." Héc arranges vegetables on a platter. "I don't remember what it's called. Something about a problem like Maria."

Rene moves around the counter and wraps her arms around me, putting her chin on my head. "It will be okay, Ramon."

My family is fairly touchy. There's no such thing as a personal space bubble around the Hernández clan. But that's not why Rene is hugging me now. Were creatures make my family look standoffish. They touch *a lot.* So even though we turn into different things, Rene was hugging me so that my bear knew we had back up and support. We were not alone. It's an odd but nice feeling.

There's a quiet knock on the door—almost hesitant. My uncle answered it and escorted my father's very skittish-looking wife through the door, and I tried to understand how he could have found someone so very different from my mother. Mamá is, well, a bear. She will leave you alone if you don't bother her, but if you go after her cubs, you're over. Tansy, which was apparently her name, reminded me more of a bunny. Big, hazel eyes, wide and blinking too much because her bangs kept getting in the way. She looked fragile and delicate, like she was spun from crystalized honey.

Rene got Tansy settled and brought her a glass of water and slid the veggie plate in front of her to snack on. Once that was done, I straightened. Now it was time for me to be the adult. For the record, when you have to tell yourself that, it's a sure sign that the thing you have to do is going to suck.

I cleared my throat and handed Tansy the package. It was thin and giftwrapped in the kind of hideous pastel wrapping paper people saved for babies. Gabi had wound a shiny ribbon around the whole thing, the curls trembling as I handed the package wordlessly to Tansy. There was the briefest pause before she took it, like it might be something terrible inside. Like I might be the kind of horrible person who would go through all this just to humiliate her. Made me wonder what kind of things Papa had told her about us.

She opened it slowly, taking care to not rip the paper. Then it floated to the floor, forgotten as she stared at the delicate silver frame in her hands—the one that had taken me and my sisters an hour to decide on. The frame held five ovals big enough for five 4x6 photos. We'd had to get the matting cut special to get five exactly. Four of the spots were already taken up with pictures of babies in various states between squalling (me) and sleeping (Gabi). Rosa looked wide eyed at the camera and Selena looked like she wanted to punch something. Mom said she was probably pooping.

"I thought." I cleared my throat and began again. "If you wanted, you could hang this in the baby's room. That way, you know, it could see us and know." Know that they weren't alone. That if my papa pulled the same crap on his new family, that Tansy wouldn't have to do it by herself. We'd all be there, the Hernández clan in all its overwhelming glory.

Tansy traced the picture of Gabi with one finger before pressing the tips of her fingers to her mouth. After a long moment, she let her hand fall. "Do you think, maybe, I could have another set? When you're older? I could put them next to each other." She didn't look at me when she said it. "I think it will be good. For the baby." Her voice was steadier on the last bit.

"I think we can manage that," I said. I held out my hand for her to shake. "I'm Ramon."

She ignored my hand and pulled me tight, still clutching the frame. "Thank you," she whispered.

Tansy pulled back, taking the dishcloth from Rene to wipe her eyes. "I'm so sorry. I'm not usually this emotional." She laughed. "Stupid hormones." She handed the cloth back to Rene.

"We always knew when my mom was pregnant," Rene said. "She'd get so angry watching Wheel of Fortune she'd throw things at Pat Sajack."

"It was hardly Pat's fault," Héctor said.

"Don't tell my mama that. Not if you want to live." Rene folded the towel and pulled a wrapped package out of a cupboard where she'd hidden it. "From us. We weren't sure what you had, so there's a gift receipt in there."

Tansy's cheeks were rosy as she opened up a box full of tiny shirts, pajamas and socks. We started asking questions about the baby and the pregnancy and conversation was slow at first, but the longer she stayed, the more relaxed Tansy became. Soon we were talking and laughing, swapping family stories that she soaked up like a sponge. And I realized that Tansy was probably hearing about most of this for the first time, and she'd been craving this connection. All of my doubts about my choices, they evaporated.

And the longer she talked, the less I saw of the bunny. Somewhere, deep down inside, Tansy is a bear. I'm only guessing, but I think that once the baby lets loose that first, long wail, that bear will rise to the surface to protect her cub. And even if I'm wrong and that doesn't happen, it doesn't matter. Because I will be there—always. Gentle and quiet and solid for the bad times, and growling and fierce for the worse times. I might never really talk to my dad again, but this baby deserves the best that I can give it. Sammy was right. It's the only way I can live with myself. The only way I know how to be.

END

About the Author

Lish McBride is the author of *Hold Me Closer, Necromancer*, *Necromancing the Stone*, *Firebug,* and *Pyromantic*, and the Tor.com Originals *Heads Will Roll* and *Burnt Sugar*.

She is also a bookseller, insomniac, and an aspiring wizard. You can follow her antics on Instagram, Twitter, Facebook and Patreon, but be prepared for her to talk about kittens. A lot.

CPSIA information can be obtained
at www.ICGtesting.com
Printed in the USA
FFOW04n0804040217
31985FF